For Mike T. and Mama D.
—Alice Faye Duncan

To Jesus Christ and Breia.
—Phyllis Dooley

In loving memory of those who passed in 2004.
Daddy, Ella, Valerie Bowers, and my nephew, Troy Spivey.
Thanks to my models: LaClaudia Marquita Williams, Cydnee Cierra Jones,
Phoenix Abraham Thompson, and Denise Darcell Campbell
—Jan Spivey Gilchrist

zonderkidz
The children's group
of Zondervan

www.zonderkidz.com

Christmas Soup
Copyright © 2005 by Alice Faye Duncan and Phyllis Dooley
Illustrations © 2005 by Jan Spivey Gilchrist

Requests for information should be addressed to:
Grand Rapids, Michigan 49530

Library of Congress Cataloging-in-Publication Data

Dooley, Phyllis.
  Christmas soup / Phyllis Dooley and Alice Faye Duncan.
      p. cm.
   Summary: When the Beenes, a family so poor that they have nothing but
watery soup for their Christmas dinner, share their food with a homeless
woman and child, they are all transformed by the selfless act.
  ISBN 0-310-70930-X (hardcover)
  [1. Sharing–Fiction. 2. Homeless persons–Fiction. 3. Poor–Fiction. 4. Christian
life–Fiction. 5. Christmas–Fiction.] I. Duncan, Alice Faye. II. Title.
  PZ7.D72653Ch 2005

[E]–dc22

                                                              2004008339

Editor: Amy De Vries
Art direction & design: Laura Maitner-Mason

Illustrations used in this book were created gouache and pastel.
The body text for this book is set in Old Claude Regular.

Printed in China

05 06 07 08 09 /TPC/ 10 9 8 7 6 5 4 3 2 1

Christmas Soup

Alice Faye Duncan and Phyllis Dooley

Illustrated by Jan Spivey Gilchrist

zonderkidz

Most of all,

love one another deeply.

Love erases many sins by forgiving them.

Welcome others into your homes without complaining.

– *1 Peter 4:8-9*

J ack Beene's belly grumbled and growled.
"Hey, Mama," he asked, "what's for dinner?"
"Christmas soup," she answered.

Yuck!" Jack said. "It's the same old watered-down soup every year."
"Aren't you hungry, honey?" Mama asked.
Jack replied, "Not for Christmas soup."

W hat's your problem?" asked Nettie Jean.
"I'm starving," answered Jack, "and I'm sick of soup."
"We know," said Baby Fannie. "Maybe we should pray
for something more this year."

Whatever," hissed Jack.
    "Dear Lord," prayed Baby Fannie out loud,
"thank you for Christmas soup.
  And please bless us with something more this year.
  In Jesus' name we pray. Amen."
    Jack rolled his eyes.
      "You pray the same thing every year,"
      he said, "and nothing ever happens."

Jack pressed his face to the cold glass and breathed 'til the window turned frosty.
Suddenly something moved on their sidewalk.
"Hey," he shouted. "Somebody's coming.
Maybe it's the pizza man."
Bam! Bam! Bam! sounded a knock at the door.

Something smells real good," said the woman.
"It's nothing but Christmas soup," said Jack.
"Just plain, old, watered down, red tomato soup."
"Mmmm," said the little boy. "Could we have some?"
"Of course," said Mama. "Guests in this house always eat first."

$\mathcal{M}$ama pulled the big door open wide.

Jack whistled. "Nope," he said. "That's not pizza."

"May we come in?" asked the woman.

"We're on our way to the homeless shelter but too tired to walk another step."

"Of course," said Mama. "After all, it's Christmas Eve."

Mama Beene filled a bowl and handed it to the little boy.
He slurped it down and gushed,
"I love it! I never had Christmas soup before!"
He wiped his face with a sleeve.
Mama filled another bowl for the woman.
She drank it all down then said,
"It's delicious."

The strangers raised their bowls for more,
again and again, until they were full.
"Look at their faces," whispered Jack.
"They look totally different," Baby Fannie whispered back.

Thank you," said the woman.
"Before we found your home,
people slammed doors in our faces."
"You're welcome," Mama Beene said.
"We don't have much at the holidays,
but there's always Christmas soup."

$\mathcal{G}$ood-bye," Jack called.

"Good-bye," Baby Fannie echoed.

"Merry Christmas, everybody," yelled the little boy.

"And God bless you and your children," said the woman.

"I believe he already has," said Mama Beene.

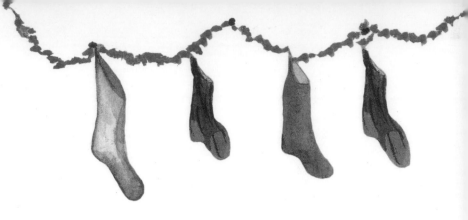

When they sat back down to finish their dinner,
Jack prayed, "Thanks, God, for everything you give us.
Even Christmas soup."